Jingle the Brass

Jingle the Brass

Patricia Newman

Pictures by **Michael Chesworth**

FARRAR, STRAUS AND GIROUX • NEW YORK

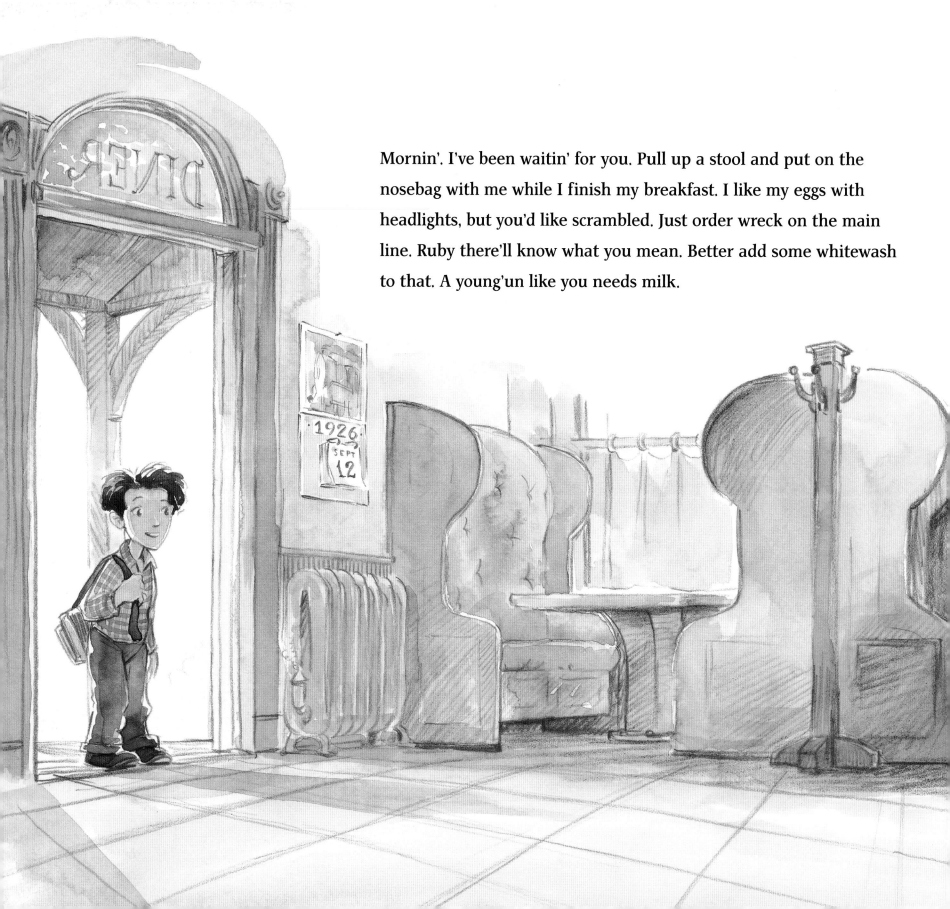

Mornin'. I've been waitin' for you. Pull up a stool and put on the nosebag with me while I finish my breakfast. I like my eggs with headlights, but you'd like scrambled. Just order wreck on the main line. Ruby there'll know what you mean. Better add some whitewash to that. A young'un like you needs milk.

Welcome to the yard. This straight track running right through the middle is the ladder.

See those cars lined up on that spur track? That's our train. All she needs is an engine. And we're fixin' to get one out of the roundhouse—see? Over there beyond the water tower.

Round-
house →

Water Tower

← Spur Track →

This here's my ole hog—number 417. I sure do love her, but sometimes she's an ornery ole gal. Climb aboard and ride the point.

Meet Joe, my ashcat. He keeps the fire burnin' so this ole hog'll have enough steam to get us where we're going. She's so temperamental. Watch Joe spoon-feed black diamonds into her firebox. That coal will glow red-hot.

The roundhouse boss says it's time to pull out onto the merry-go-round. Wave to Mabel, the merry-go-round operator. She'll line us up with the outbound track so we can hitch up to our train.

Before we hitch up, let's stop and give her a drink.
She sure is thirsty.

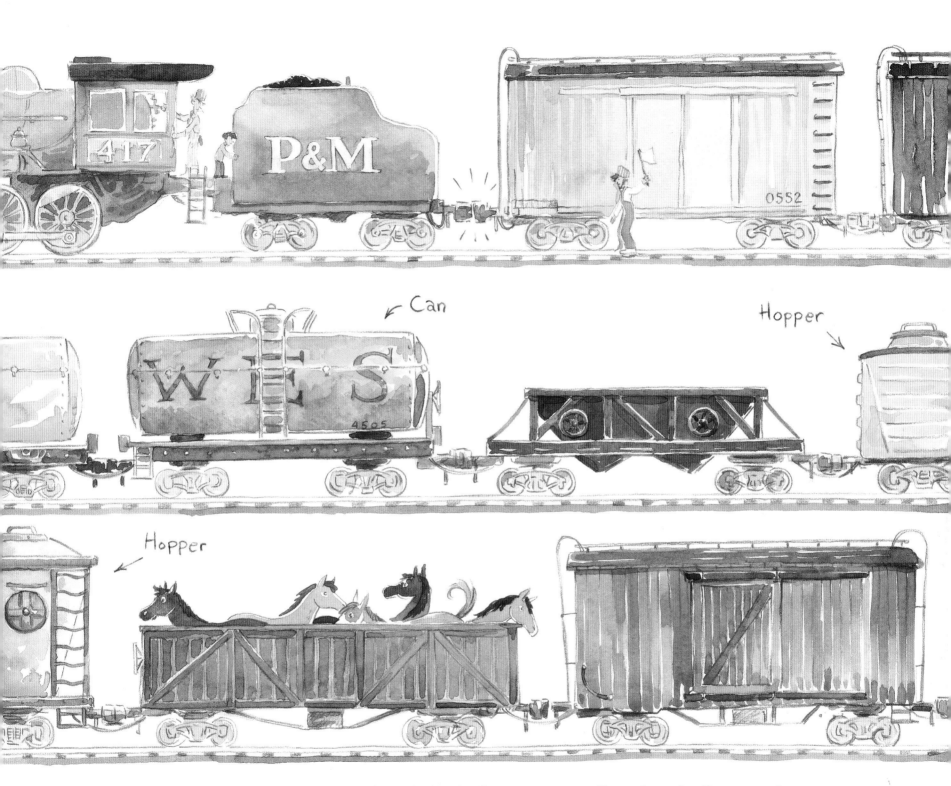

We've got ourselves a jigger today—that's the heaviest train allowed on the line. Conductor says we got grain in the hoppers, oil in the cans . . .

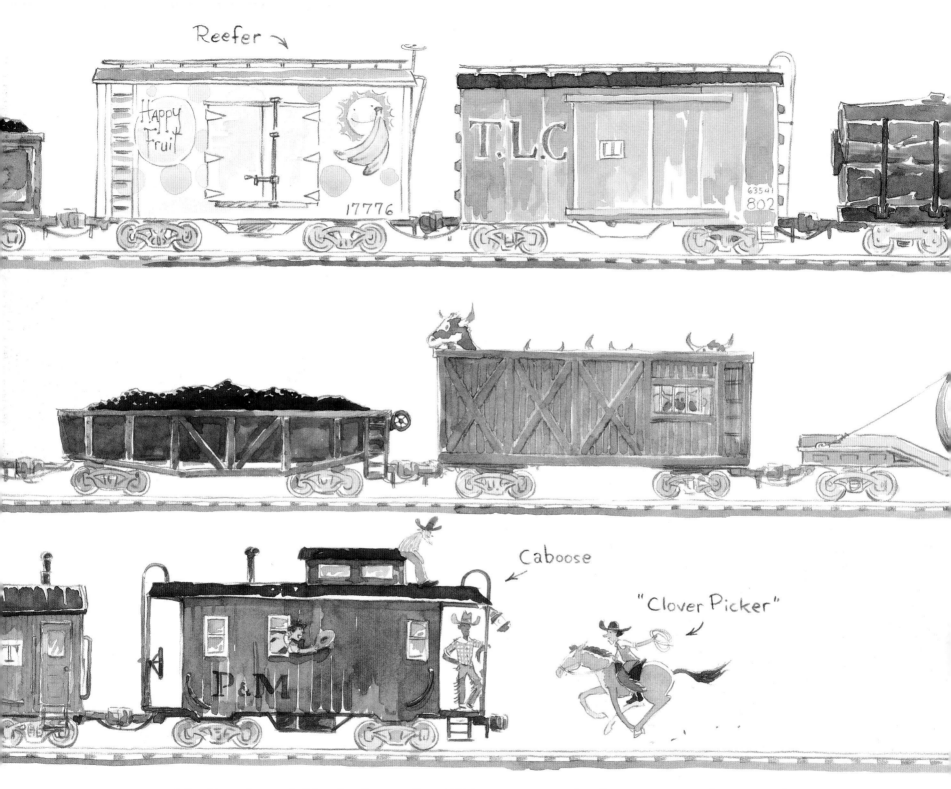

. . . and fruit and vegetables in the reefers. We're even carrying honest-to-goodness cowboys in the caboose. Them clover pickers will drive the cattle on and off the livestock cars.

My ticker says it's time to shove off. Jingle the brass to let the rear brakeman know we're leaving the station. Conductor says we're over a mile long today!

That semaphore there says to slow down and proceed with caution. Must be something on the tracks up ahead. Ole hoggers like me are called eagle eyes because we have to keep a sharp eye out for anything in our way. Don't want a cornfield meet, now, do we? What's a cornfield meet, you say? Why, that's a head-on train wreck.

"Go"

"Caution"

"Stop"

"A Cornfield Meet"

Looks like we got ourselves some gandy dancers fixin' up a bit of track.

Lean out the window. Can you hear 'em singin'?

Usually we don't allow passengers on a freight
train, but you watch as we approach this here trestle. See
them hoboes climbing the hill and nailing her on the fly?
The railroad bulls will arrest them for sure. The bulls are
ridin' this train undercover today, hidin' in the boxcars.

A semaphore tells me to pick up new orders on the fly. Ole Joe here sticks his arm out and hooks it through a hoop while the train is moving. He grabs our flimsies typed out all nice and neat. Watch him now. Be sure he doesn't fumble the hoop.

The track curves this way and that for the next few miles. Look behind us. The brakemen are ridin' out to inspect each car for sticking brakes. The curves give them a good view.

There's a tunnel up ahead, but don't worry about the brakemen up on top.

They know what to do. See those telltales hanging in front of the tunnel?

When the brakemen feel those ropes brush their backs, they hit the deck until
we're clear of the tunnel.

Our new orders say to pull off the main line at this here siding, and sit in the hole while a passenger train rolls by. Nothin' I hate more than lying dead.

Oooh-wee! Look at all that varnish speedin' by. If you were on the plush, you could sleep in the snoozer and put on the nosebag in the diner.

We're on our way again. I love the wind in my face.
Stick your head out the window. The rods are flashing now!

Seems like we're only just gettin' started again, but we need to stop at the next station. Joe and I'll treat you to a donut at Sally's hash house. Best rolling stock on the line, eh, Joe?

This is the end of the line for you, pal. Thanks for the company. I've got to work a little longer, but your trick is up. Time for you to pull the pin and go home.

That westbound train is deadheading back to the station—see all the empty cars? Mighty fine knowin' you. Your conductor's callin'. Best be on your way.

All aboard!

Ashcat: A locomotive fireman who stokes the fire so the water will boil and make steam.

Black diamonds: Coal.

Boxcars: Roofed freight cars with sliding doors.

Brakeman: The workhorse of the train. He connects, inspects, and tests the air brakes, protects the rear of the train if it is stopped on the track, throws switches, and cuts cars out of the train at the appropriate stations.

Caboose: The last car in a freight train. Also the office and lunchroom for the train crew.

Cans: Tank cars.

Clover pickers: Cowboys transporting a shipment of cattle by train.

Conductor: On a freight train, the conductor keeps track of the paperwork for all the goods on the train to be sure they are delivered properly.

Cornfield meet: Either a head-on collision or one narrowly averted. Because train tracks ran through all kinds of fields—corn, wheat, etc.—engineers used the cornfield in their expression.

Deadhead(ing): Empty train cars being transported to another station; a railroad worker who finishes his shift at one station and rides back home on a free pass.

Diner: The dining car on a passenger train.

Eagle eye: A sharp-eyed engineer always on the lookout for signals and obstacles on the tracks.

Eggs with headlights: Eggs sunny-side up.

Engine: The car at the head end of the train that supplies the power. The engine in this book is modeled after the Union Pacific 4466 locomotive, popular in the 1920s. It is currently retired at the California State Railroad Museum in Sacramento, California.

Flimsies: Orders typed on extremely thin paper.

Fumble the hoop: New train orders were attached to a hoop and held up for the fireman on a moving train. The fireman was supposed to hook his arm through the hoop and bring the orders aboard. If the fireman missed, he fumbled the hoop.

Gandy dancers: Track workers.

Give her a drink: Fill the tender with water.

Hash house: A railroad lunchroom or restaurant.

Hoboes: Migratory workers or tramps who hop on trains for free transportation from place to place.

Hog: An engine.

Hoggers: Engineers (also **hog eye** or **hoghead**).

Hoppers: Steel-sided railroad cars that can be loaded from the top and emptied from the bottom.

In the hole: Waiting on a siding.

Jigger: The heaviest train allowed on the main line.

Jingle the brass: Ring the bell; blow the whistle.

Ladder: The main track in the railroad yard.

Lying dead: At a complete stop.

Main line: The main north–south or east–west track.

Merry-go-round: The turntable in front of the roundhouse.

Nail her on the fly: Hop aboard a moving train.

On the plush: To ride in a passenger train (also **on the velvet**).

Pull the pin: Quit work and go home.

Put on the nosebag: To eat.

Railroad bulls: Railroad police.

Reefers: Refrigerator cars.

Ride the point: To ride in a locomotive.

Riding out: To ride on top of a boxcar.

Rods are flashing: The rods drive the wheel of a locomotive; the faster they move, the faster the engine goes; when the rods are flashing, the train is moving very fast; if the engineer leans far enough out the window in the cab, he can actually see the rods flashing.

Rolling stock: Donuts.

Roundhouse: A circular garage where locomotives are cleaned, serviced, and repaired.

Semaphore: A track-side signal.

Siding: A piece of track used by trains to get off the main line and out of the way of a faster train.

Snoozer: A car with sleeping compartments.

Spoon: A fireman's shovel.

Spur track: A dead-end side track used for repairs or railroad cars waiting to be coupled to a train.

Telltales: Dangling ropes hanging in front of a tunnel; a reminder to brakemen on top of the train to duck their heads at the tunnel entrance.

Ticker: A railroader's pocket watch.

Trestle: A bridge with railroad tracks.

Trick: A railroad worker's shift.

Varnish: Passenger cars; the first passenger cars were highly lacquered to make them shine.

Whitewash: Milk.

Wreck on the main line: Scrambled eggs.

Yard: A system of tracks for storing and building cars, and for assembling, or making up, trains.

To Ken, Elise, and Scott for believing in me —P.N.
To Utah Phillips —M.C.

Author's Note

Special thanks to Al Shelley (former Southern Pacific hogger) and the staff and docents
at the California State Railroad Museum for helping me reconstruct and, in a small way, resurrect
the age of steam that was alive and well in 1926. Additional thanks to Connie Goldsmith
for her wisdom and support; Karen Grencik for finding the right people to love this book;
and Wesley Adams and Michael Chesworth for giving it life.
If you'd like to read more about railroads and the way they work, try *Eyewitness Books: Train* (New
York, Alfred A. Knopf, 1992) and *Train Talk: An Illustrated Guide to Lights, Hand Signals, Whistles and
Other Languages of Railroading* by Roger Yepsen (New York: Pantheon, 1983).

www.fsgkidsbooks.com

Library of Congress Cataloging-in-Publication Data
Newman, Patricia.
  Jingle the brass : Patricia Newman ; pictures by Michael Chesworth.— 1st ed.
    p. cm.
  Summary: On a train trip, an engineer teaches a boy the expressions used by
railroad workers as he describes the different kinds of cars, freight, and people
they see.
  ISBN 0-374-33679-2
  [1. Railroads—Terminology—Fiction. 2. Railroads—Trains—Fiction. 3. Voyages
and travels—Fiction.] I. Chesworth, Michael, ill. II. Title.

PZ7.N4854Ji 2004
[E]—dc21
                                                                    2003048055